Contents

Gabby
GHOST HUNTER

The Ghost in the Castle

by Stephanie Faris

raintree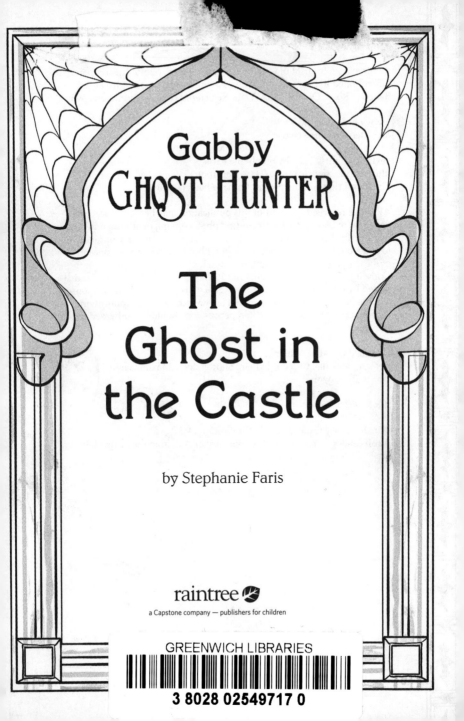

a Capstone company — publishers for children

Raintree is an imprint of Capstone Global Library Limited, a company
incorporated in England and Wales having its registered office at 264
Banbury Road, Oxford, OX2 7DY – Registered company number: 6695582

www.raintree.co.uk
myorders@raintree.co.uk

Designed by Jaime Willems
Design Elements: Chloe Friedlein; Shutterstock: Maxim Gaigul,
Wasan Ritthawon

978 1 3982 5505 0

British Library Cataloguing in Publication Data
A full catalogue record for this book is available from the British Library.

Printed and bound in India.

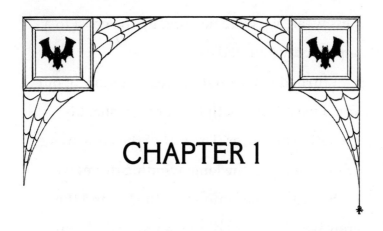

CHAPTER 1

There was a castle right in front of me – an actual castle. It almost didn't look real. But not only was it real, I'd be going inside in just a few minutes – along with the rest of the *Ghost Search* crew.

Ghost Search, my dad's podcast, was the reason I was here. In each week's episode, Dad investigated some of the most haunted places in the country. I was spending the summer travelling with him and his crew.

This week, we were heading up the coast to a supposedly haunted castle.

I turned to look out the rear window of our van. I was riding with Dad and Keisha, his executive producer. The rest of the crew was following us up the long, winding driveway.

Spending the summer with Dad and the crew was fun, but I didn't get too caught up in the hauntings. If you asked me, there was always a scientific explanation for things.

"Is this actually real?" Dad asked as our van slowed to a stop.

At first I thought he was as impressed with the castle as I was. But when I spun back round, I realized it wasn't the castle that had caught Dad's attention. It was the woman standing on the front porch. She was ghostly pale, wore a long white dress and held a lantern.

She's really taking this ghost thing seriously, I thought, smirking. I didn't believe in ghosts.

In fact, I spent most of our investigations trying to debunk the hauntings.

Dad already seemed unhappy with the woman's get-up, though, so I kept my thoughts to myself. Instead I said, "Did you know this place sat empty for eighty years before the current owner bought it?"

I often helped out by researching the places we visited. I'd used Dad's tablet to look up the history of the castle during the drive. "The owner turned it into a tourist attraction," I added. "People pay to come and look round it."

"We don't pay." Dad looked over at Keisha. "Remind me to mention that on the episode."

Keisha and Dad both stepped out of the van. I grabbed my backpack and reached for the handle to open the back door, not taking my eyes off the woman on the porch. Even though I knew she wasn't a ghost, she looked pretty spooky.

"Good evening," the woman said as we walked towards her. She held up the lantern in her hand.

"Hi," Dad said. "You must be the owner." He turned, looking over my head, and waved. I knew that was for the crew. He wanted them to record our arrival for the episode.

The woman nodded. "I'm Michelle Wagner. I'll be your host this evening," she continued. She moved her left arm in a dramatic sweeping gesture towards the castle. "Lewis Ludwig built this castle in 1853 for his wife, who loved castles. He built this front section first so they could live here during construction."

"My research says she never really got to live here, though," I interrupted.

Everyone – including Dad – turned and looked at me. Dad was frowning, and I knew where I'd gone wrong. I was supposed to let the host tell the story.

"Yes, the young lady is right," Michelle said, keeping her same neutral expression. "Grace Ludwig was expecting her first child when she and Lewis moved in. Then, one day, she went into labour."

I wanted to pull the notepad out of my backpack and take notes so I didn't forget anything. But I was afraid if I did, I'd break the spell. So I made mental notes instead: *Lewis Ludwig. Grace Ludwig. 1853.*

"They called the midwife to deliver the baby," Michelle continued. "But a storm rolled in, preventing her from getting to the castle. Unfortunately, neither Grace nor the baby made it."

"That's so tragic," I said quietly.

Dad gave me a sad smile before turning back to Michelle. "Tell us a little about the paranormal activity here," he said.

"To this day employees and visitors report

hearing a phone ringing throughout the castle," she said. "We believe it's Grace, trying to reach her husband from beyond the grave." She turned. "Let's head inside."

Keisha and the rest of the crew followed her. Dad started to follow, but I tugged his sleeve to stop him. He turned to face me.

"She's a little . . . over the top, don't you think?" I said. "I mean, with the outfit and everything?"

Dad shrugged. "I don't disagree," he said. "But at least it makes things interesting. And we can always edit out what we don't want."

"But it's not authentic," I argued. "Listeners might think she's putting on an act for the show."

Authentic was Dad's fancy word for *real*. I knew it was important to him that we took this seriously. We needed listeners to trust us. That was the only way any of this worked.

"That's why we're here," he reminded me. "To prove whether or not this place is haunted. We'll find out if the noises people hear really are from Grace's ghost."

Dad might have said *we*. But I knew he hoped we'd find something that couldn't be disproved. Some proof that the hauntings were real. I was here to debunk.

"Let's go," Dad said, starting up the stairs. "We don't want to miss the tour."

"Wait!" I exclaimed.

Dad stopped again. He turned to look at me.

"I still get to stay for the investigation tonight, right?" I asked.

I held my breath, waiting for his answer. Most of Dad's investigations took place late at night. That meant he usually sent me to bed before they started.

But this time, we were staying at a hotel more than thirty minutes away. Dad had agreed it would be easier to let me stay on site rather than sending me back to the hotel.

"You're staying," Dad said. "But remember the rules."

I nodded. "Stay with the group and keep an open mind."

Dad smiled. "Exactly. Let's go."

I'd do my best to keep those promises, but I also had a job to do – and that involved finding out what was really going on at Ludwig Castle. Sometimes that meant breaking the rules a little.

Notes

If you want to see a haunted castle in person, visit Glamis Castle in Angus, Scotland. Over 600 years old, the castle is reported to have at least nine ghosts roaming around in it!

One of the ghosts that has been seen for centuries is a cheeky little pageboy. The story goes that he was always getting into trouble. As a punishment for his misdeeds, he would be told to sit on a stone seat in the corridor outside the living room.

One cold winter's night, the pageboy was told to sit on the stone seat. Nobody remembered at bedtime that he was still there. In the morning, he was found frozen to death. His ghost has been spotted still sitting there...

Today, you can tour the castle. While you can't spend the night, it still sounds fun to visit. See how many ghosts you can spot!

CHAPTER 2

Getting to see the place we'd be investigating was always one of my favourite parts. It was my job to take notes so I could research later.

Michelle led us to the study first. The room was filled with old-fashioned furniture and a bookcase. I wanted to creep away from the group and see what books were on the shelves, but not as much as I wanted to hear the stories Michelle was telling us.

"Before TVs and computers, people would sit in here and read for hours," she said, sweeping her hand to the left like a person in a car advert. "It's what they did for fun."

People – including me – still sat and read for hours. But now wasn't the time to mention that. Especially as one of the microphone operators was recording everything for the podcast. I didn't think Dad's listeners wanted to hear about my hobbies.

Michelle led us into a giant room in the middle of the castle. It was one of the most beautiful rooms I'd ever seen. Stained-glass windows stretched all the way to the tall ceilings. The floor was made of marble, and a massive table lined with chairs filled the room.

"Cast your gaze upon the Great Hall," Michelle said, motioning with her arm as she walked backwards. "If the Ludwigs had moved in as planned, this would have been where they entertained their guests. There's a kitchen back here too. Follow me."

We followed her to a door in the far-left corner. Through the doorway was a small kitchen. It was like no kitchen I'd ever seen. It had a checked floor and striped wallpaper but no fridge, oven or microwave.

"It doesn't look like much cooking happens in here," I said.

"It was designed to feed crowds, but it's been empty as long as I've owned it," Michelle said. "No one lives here full time, so it didn't seem worth it to put in any appliances."

"What happened after Grace died?" I asked. "Didn't her husband live here?"

Michelle shook her head. "He was too heartbroken. The property changed hands a few times in the late 1800s, but then it sat empty for a long, long time."

I frowned. *Wouldn't the people who lived here in the 1800s still cook?* I thought. *This had to have been a kitchen people used at some point.*

"Where do the crying sounds people hear come from?" Dad asked, changing the subject.

"Upstairs in the main bedroom," Michelle said. "I'll show you." She led us back to the main hallway, then took a left towards the staircase.

"Grace's ghost is also called the Lady in White," she called back to us.

"Let me guess," I said. "She's always wearing a white dress when she's spotted?"

Reports of a Lady in White were common at so many haunted places. It seemed like there'd be at least one ghost wearing a different colour – a Lady in Purple or a Man in Orange.

"That's right," Michelle answered, ignoring my sarcasm. "Careful on the stairs."

We got to the top of the stairs and followed Michelle to the left. The main bedroom was another huge room. It had big, spooky windows with rounded tops and straight bottoms.

Michelle lifted her lantern to give us a little light. "This is the main bedroom," she said. "And this –" She moved her lantern so it lit up the wall behind her. "– is Grace Ludwig."

It took me a second to realize she was talking about a painting hanging on the wall to my right. The woman in the painting wasn't smiling. In fact, she looked almost . . . angry.

I jotted down some notes: Dark hair, dark eyes, pointy nose and chin.

"All of our reported sightings of Grace are in this room," Michelle said.

"Who reports the sightings?" Dad asked. "Have you seen her yourself?"

Michelle nodded. "Several times, actually. You can clearly make out a white dress, similar to the one I'm wearing now. Many others have seen her over the years too. Families who've lived here, guests who've visited . . . I have a small team of employees who are in and out of this room quite a bit. It spooks just about everyone."

I looked around the room. A four-poster bed sat in the centre of the space. Dark wood nightstands and a dresser completed the space. I concluded it had all been placed there so tourists could imagine what it had looked like when Grace was alive.

"Where exactly do people see the Lady in White?" I asked.

Michelle pointed to a door opposite the one we'd come through. "Over there, near the door."

"Anything else about this room?" Dad asked.

Michelle nodded again. "My employees have also reported hearing a phone ring in here. Not a mobile phone, either. An old-fashioned phone that sounds like a bicycle bell."

I didn't know how old-fashioned phones sounded. We didn't even have a house phone. And my bicycle at home didn't have a bell.

I made a note to do some research on that piece of the story.

"Legend has it that after Grace died, the phone would ring at all hours of the day and night." Michelle turned and looked directly at me. "It was Grace Ludwig, trying to reach her husband."

Silence fell over the room. I saw Dad and Keisha exchange a look. The story was spooky. But then I remembered something.

"I thought you said he didn't move in, though," I pointed out.

Michelle glanced back at Dad before turning her frown back on me. "Sorry?"

"You said the phone rang at all hours of the day and night," I reminded her. "But Grace's husband was supposedly too heartbroken to live here without her. Wouldn't someone need to be here to hear the phone ringing? And answer it?"

Michelle stared at me, not saying anything. She clearly didn't appreciate me poking holes in her ghost story.

"You know, I think we can take it from here," Dad interjected. "Keisha, do you want to see Michelle out? Maybe get the keys to the place in case we need them?"

At that, our host's expression softened. I could tell she was relieved to be finished and heading home for the night. Dad always requested the hosts leave before we started investigating. That way we knew we were truly alone and wouldn't have any interference.

Keisha turned to Michelle. "I'll walk you out," she said.

After they left, Dad turned to the rest of the crew. "Let's start in the study," he said.

I didn't have to be told twice. I followed the crew out of the bedroom. I had an investigation to start – and debunking to do.

Notes

It took a long time for telephones to make their way into homes. It all started in the mid-1800s, when an Italian inventor called Antonio Meucci came up with the idea for a "talking telegraph". Before then, a telegraph was the quickest way to get a message across a long distance, as post could take a long time to reach people.

While Meucci came up with the first basic telephone in 1849, his invention never became official. Scottish-born scientist Alexander Graham Bell is considered the inventor of the telephone. He received the first patent for it in 1876, in the United States.

In 1912, the first public phone boxes were introduced. They were made of wood. By the 1930s, rich householders had their own landline phones at home. By the 1980s, the cordless phone was becoming popular. Now, most people use their mobile phones instead of landline phones. But businesses continue to use them.

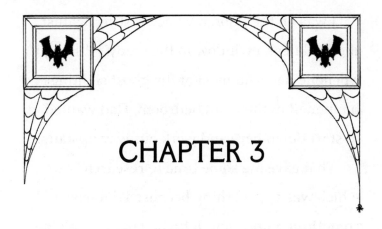

CHAPTER 3

"Are you looking for your husband?" Dad asked the question and waited. Silence.

That was typical, though. The goal wasn't necessarily for us to hear something *now*. The goal was for the recorder in Dad's hand to capture something we'd hear later.

EVPs – electronic voice phenomena – were a huge part of every investigation. Sometimes the recorders picked up weird sounds, like breathing or footsteps. But also they'd capture a word or even a few words.

I was on the floor, my back resting against the wall near a window in the study. Although Michelle had said most of the ghost sightings happened in the main bedroom, Dad wanted to start down here and work our way upstairs.

That gave me some time to research, which was a good thing because I'd uncovered something important. It turned out that phones hadn't been invented until the 1870s. I stared at the tablet in my hands. I hadn't even looked all that hard to find the information.

I knew from my earlier research that the castle had been built in the 1850s. And Michelle had told us Grace Ludwig died shortly afterwards. Unless ghosts kept up with changing technology, it didn't seem likely she'd have been calling her husband. She wouldn't even have known about phones.

"My batteries are dying," Keisha said from across the main hallway. She held a second recorder on the other side of the room in case noise came from that direction.

I hopped up. "I'll go and get more." I'd take any chance to do some exploring on my own.

"Gabs," Dad said, stopping me as I made my way across the room. "You know how I feel about you running around strange places alone."

"We're the only ones here," Keisha pointed out. "Michelle promised we'd have the place to ourselves when she left."

"I'm just going to the Great Hall." I pointed in that direction. The Great Hall was just a short walk down a corridor, to the left. "That's where all the equipment is, right?"

"Actually . . ." Keisha looked sheepish. "I left the batteries in my backpack. It's upstairs."

"It's no big deal," I insisted. "I can get it."

Dad looked at me, and I braced myself for the "no" that was coming. But he took a deep breath, then let it out again.

"Fine," he said. "Take the tablet with you, just in case you see something."

I grinned. This was a good, good sign. Dad was so protective. Okay, yeah, I was basically locked in the castle, so it wasn't like anything could happen. But still, it felt like progress.

I grabbed the tablet with one hand and my backpack with the other. I slung the bag over my shoulder. My notepad was inside it. That's where I'd written down my notes on the Lady in White – her background, where people claimed to have seen her. Going upstairs would give me the perfect chance to look for her.

I'd be quick. Dad wouldn't even miss me.

I entered the corridor and was surrounded by darkness. Off in the distance, I heard crew members shuffling around as they worked to set up the equipment. Tomorrow we'd use it to go over all the stuff we recorded tonight.

I passed the Great Hall – where most of the crew was – and kept walking towards the stairs. Only they weren't there.

I paused and tried to remember the route we'd taken. We'd gone from the hallway to the study to the Great Hall. Then we'd come down this very corridor. The hallway was at the end of it, and the stairs were just there in front of the door.

I just had to keep going.

I was relieved when the corridor opened into the entrance hall. Getting lost in a big, creepy castle wouldn't be fun.

Now that I'd got my bearings, I used the tablet to shoot some video of the corridors. Not that there was anything really worth recording. The corridors were a little spooky, but mostly just quiet and dark. But Dad liked to have footage of us walking around, and I'd totally bombed that part of things.

I was starting towards the stairs, tablet in front of me and camera running, when a sound caught my attention. It wasn't the crew. I could no longer hear them. Maybe Dad had shushed them. He sometimes did that when he was trying to do EVP work.

Off in the distance was a sound I hadn't heard before – at least not in here. I held my breath, afraid to make any noise.

Ring-ring-ring.

My bicycle didn't have a bell, but if it did, it would probably sound like . . . that. But I knew there were no bicycles in the castle. Did that mean . . .? Yes, that had to be the sound of an old phone ringing.

Notes

A man called Raymond Bayless first looked into EVPs in 1959. But as sound recording became more popular, other experts started noticing voices in those recordings. One of those people was Friedrich Jürgenson. He was playing a recording of bird songs when he thought he heard his father and his wife — only they were both dead.

In 1982, paranormal researcher Sarah Estep started an organization called the American Association of Electronic Voice Phenomena. The organization still exists today. There are also many online groups who share their own EVPs.

Although paranormal investigators often use EVPs as proof that ghosts exist, scientists have another explanation — auditory pareidolia. That's where your brain looks for patterns in the static heard in silence. But some EVPs can sound eerily real.

CHAPTER 4

Ring-ring-ring. Ring-ring-ring. The sound continued. At first I'd thought it was coming from down the corridor, but now it sounded like it was coming from upstairs.

I glanced down at the tablet to make sure it was still recording. I needed to capture this sound. I just hoped the ringing would be clear enough.

It wasn't easy to walk up those stairs while still holding the tablet in front of me so I walked very carefully. The stairs were super steep. Each one felt like it was metres high compared to modern stairs.

I was so busy trying not to trip, I forgot I was all alone on a staircase in a strange castle. That hit me once I got to the top step. The staircase was chilly and dark, and it seemed like every time I moved, shadows moved all around me.

Ring-ring.

I heard it again, only this time it was different. There were two rings, then silence.

After a long pause to listen, I continued on. The sound was coming from this floor. I was sure of it.

First things first, though. Entering the main bedroom, I spotted Keisha's backpack in the corner of the room. I walked over, unzipped the top and pulled out some batteries. I slipped them into my back pocket, then turned around.

Despite the ringing I'd just heard, things were quiet up here – so, so quiet. I looked around. No sign of a phone – just the big bedroom we'd seen on the tour. With all this silence, it felt like something bad was about to happen.

I moved across the room to examine the gigantic painting. That was Grace Ludwig. I recognized her from the historical documents I'd found in my research. All the facts online had rung true, including her date of death and the fact that her husband had built Ludwig Castle for her.

I cared about facts, not fiction.

But there was something about that painting. I couldn't look away. It felt like the woman in it was staring at me.

I moved to the left, sure that would solve it. But it didn't. The eyes seemed to follow me, even when I kept going way, way to the left.

Ghosts aren't real. Ghosts aren't real. Ghosts aren't real, I told myself over and over again.

The reassurance helped a little – but only a little. Those eyeballs still seemed to follow me across the room.

I walked closer and stared at the painting, then squatted down a little. Aha! It was easier to see up-close. It was just a trick of the eyes. Because the woman in the painting was staring straight ahead, she'd be staring at me no matter where I stood.

I stood up again and looked around the room. Lifting the tablet, I scanned the space.

"Hi, Grace," I said.

I felt weird talking to an empty room. But it felt even weirder to just stand around recording nothing. So I kept going.

"Did something bad happen in here?" I asked.

It was one of the things Dad asked when he was doing EVPs. If you could get a ghost upset, sometimes it would bring a response.

I held my breath, listening for something – anything. Suddenly, a chill spread over my body. The air around me felt different, like there was less oxygen in the room. Like someone was near by – watching me.

I turned slowly, not looking away from the tablet screen as I did. If I was going to see something, the tablet would too.

Besides, I felt safer with the tablet between me and whatever was on the other side of it. And there was definitely something on the other side of it.

My mouth fell open at what I saw on the screen. The outline of a woman was clearly visible near the doorway across the room – exactly where Michelle had said people saw the Lady in White. And what was on my screen definitely looked like a ghost.

Notes

Have you ever looked at a painting and felt like the eyes were following you? No, that doesn't mean the painting is haunted. It's actually a trick of the eye.

When it comes to flat images – like paintings, for example – your eyes see things the same way, no matter where you stand. If the painting is of a person who's looking straight ahead, that means those eyes will be staring out at you whether you're standing in front of the painting or off to the side.

Talented artists know how to use shadows and light to create depth. That's all part of learning how to paint. Since a painting is a flat surface, depth is all an illusion.

Photographers can do the same thing depending on how they light a scene. You could have a large photograph in your house with eyes that seem to follow you as you move around the room.

Even if you know the reasoning, it can seem a little creepy. Especially if you're alone in a room.

CHAPTER 5

I stared at the screen. Were my eyes playing tricks on me? No. The image was still there. And it still looked like a Lady in White.

My heart felt like it might beat right out of my chest. If I lowered the tablet, I'd be looking straight at her.

But it couldn't be a ghost. I didn't believe in ghosts.

Dad was always telling me to keep an open mind. And I tried. But I loved science and facts. I didn't love things I couldn't explain.

I took a deep breath and walked towards the outline I saw on the screen. The shape was small at the top, then got wider. That was what looked like shoulders. Then it came in a little at what looked like the waist, only to go way out at the bottom like a woman wearing one of those old-fashioned dresses with a big skirt.

I squinted as I lowered the screen a little so I could look over the top of it. The shape remained. If it was a ghost, wouldn't it –

Disappear?

That was exactly what happened with my next step. It was as though the ghost – or whatever it was – could read my mind.

I stopped and stared. It was like a shadow, only in reverse. The shape was lighter than the area around it instead of darker.

I took one step back. That did it. The Lady in White appeared again. I repeated the movement. Yes, the "ghost" was only visible to a certain point. It disappeared when I got closer, then reappeared when I went back.

I looked around. If this was a shadow, what would be causing it? And why would the shadow be white?

Lifting the tablet, I scanned the area behind me. The painting of Grace Ludwig hung between two large windows, neither of which had curtains. Light streamed in, and as I walked closer, I saw the full moon in the sky. Its light shone directly through the window.

Quickly, like it might get away, I spun to look for the Lady in White again. Nothing. But that could be the angle.

Still holding up the tablet, I moved back to my original spot. Sure enough, as I moved back into place, the reverse-shadow appeared again.

"Yes!" I cried.

I wanted to clamp my hand over my mouth, but both hands were on the tablet. Then I remembered nobody could hear me anyway. I was up here alone.

I tapped on the screen to stop recording. Then I pulled up the phone app on the tablet and called Keisha.

Or at least that's what I tried to do. The screen said it was dialling, but nothing was happening. It was just silence on the other end.

I should have realized I wouldn't have service. I was in a castle in the middle of nowhere. I'd been in enough strange places this summer to know that in buildings like this, reception could be horrible.

I zipped up my backpack, slung it over my shoulder and started walking, holding the tablet in front of me. Eventually – hopefully – I'd get enough service to make the call.

"I should've grabbed the two-way radio," I muttered to myself as I started back down the stairs.

I tried to watch where I was going. It wasn't safe to walk down the stairs with my eyes on the screen. And besides –

Something was wonky.

I was leaning to the right. But I wasn't trying to lean to the right. It was like something was pushing me that way. Not someone, but something.

I forced myself to the left. But pushing my body to the left did nothing. In fact, I was leaning to the right even more.

I gripped the railing with my right hand. I didn't want to fall, and if this kept pushing me, I might lose my footing. And if I fell, how long would it take before Dad and Keisha came looking for me?

I forced myself to take the next step. I could do this. I could do this without falling. I didn't have a choice.

Notes

Seeing in the dark can be tricky. You might even notice that it takes a while for your eyes to adjust after the lights go out.

That's because our eyes are made up of something called rods and cones. Rods help you see in the dark. Although rods are much more efficient than cones, they take longer to switch from a lit room to a dark one.

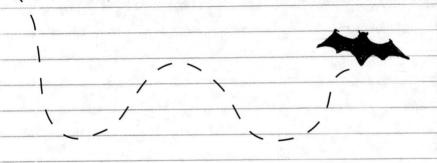

Cones are faster to adjust. They help you see when things are really, really bright. Somewhere in the middle is regular lighting, which is when both your rods and cones work together to help you see.

CHAPTER 6

The steps seemed even taller than they had on the way up. I was scared I might miss one and fall all the way to the bottom, especially with some mysterious force pushing me.

Frustration surged through me. I wasn't sure what I was fighting against. But it was enough to get me down one step, then another. Gripping the railing helped, so I gripped it harder. It made me feel safer.

Somehow – I wasn't sure how – I made it to the bottom of the stairs. I sank to the floor and stared up at the ceiling. I was beyond relieved to be back on solid footing.

Turning my head, I looked back at the stairs. I blinked and looked again. No, it wasn't my imagination. The staircase was crooked.

I lifted the tablet and started typing terms into the search box. *Crooked stairs. Feeling of being pushed. Dizziness from slanted floors.* Finally, I got somewhere.

"The funhouse effect," I read out loud. "When floors are slanted, it can throw off your inner balance. You can start to feel dizzy and off-balance. It can be easy to assume the weird feeling you have is paranormal activity when really it's just uneven flooring."

That explained why I'd felt weird on the stairs. But it had felt like more than that. It had felt like someone was pushing me. Like no matter how I fought it, that force would win.

But in the end, *I'd* won.

Just then the tablet buzzed in my hand. The screen filled with notifications. I had service again. And Keisha had been trying to reach me.

Ring-ring-ring.

I was still staring at the screen when the same old-fashioned phone noise I'd heard earlier echoed through the halls again.

Grabbing my backpack and tablet, I started in the direction of the sound. I tapped on the screen to dial Keisha as I walked.

To my surprise, Dad answered. "Where are you?" he said. "We've been calling and texting."

"Can you hear that?" I asked.

I kept going, following the long corridor in the hopes of finding the ringing. The sound could go away at any second. I needed to see if I could find the source before it stopped. If I was lucky, I'd record it on the tablet, but I couldn't always count on that. It would be better if Dad could hear it too.

"I hear you," Dad said. "Are you in the hallway?"

"The phone," I said, still holding the tablet out in front of me. "You didn't hear the phone?"

"We didn't get a call from you until now," Dad said. "We were worried about you. We've been trying to reach you."

Silence. Then I saw a form up ahead. Remembering what I'd seen upstairs, my heart started racing again.

But there was no cause for alarm. It was Dad. He stopped, and the light streaming in from the windows behind him showed me he had his arms crossed over his chest.

"Come on," Dad said. "Keisha needs those batteries, and I want you to stay close. We could do with a hand in here."

I listened intently as I followed Dad back towards the study. But the ringing sound had gone.

Notes

Your brain tells you what your eyes see. And if the two don't agree, things can get a little wonky. That's why you might get car sick in the back seat. You can't see the road as clearly as you can from the front. You're moving, but those movements don't match what your eyes see.

That's also why crooked floors can make you feel dizzy. Your eyes see things as straight, but your body is moving at a slight angle. This is known as the "funhouse effect". Funhouses often use slanted walls and floors.

As a lot of haunted places are really old, they are more likely to have crooked walls and floors. (Over time, buildings shift as the ground beneath them changes.) Plus it's easy to get caught up in a paranormal investigation. You can start to think that a weird feeling is a sign something spooky is happening.

CHAPTER 7

Ring-ring-ring.

"See?" I said excitedly. "You can hear it!"

Dad and Keisha stood on either side of me in the study. While I'd been gone, they'd continued their EVP work. They hadn't noticed anything themselves, but that didn't mean something wouldn't show up on the recording.

Now they both stared at the tablet in my hands. I'd done it. I'd captured audio of the ringing phone. We could hear it as clearly as my footsteps and voice.

Dad smiled at me. "Great work, Gabby."

Keisha smiled too, but more hesitantly. "We still need to make sure there's no other explanation for the noise," she said.

I blushed. Keisha was right. Debunking things was my job. Since when did I get so excited about evidence of ghosts that I forgot about working out the real cause of a smell, sound or weird feeling?

Since never, that was when.

"You're right," I agreed. "It doesn't mean the castle is haunted. It just means we have evidence to play on the podcast. We can talk about the ringing sound and the crooked stairs."

"What about crooked stairs?" Dad asked.

"Come with me."

I held the tablet close to my chest and started walking fast, leaving my backpack in the study.

"Slow down, Gabby," Dad called after me.

I adjusted my pace slightly but not by much. I wanted to see the stairs again myself as much as I wanted to show them to Dad and Keisha.

Soon, we stood at the bottom of the staircase. There was just enough moonlight coming in through the windows to make out the shapes of each super-tall step in front of us. They definitely weren't straight.

"See?" I motioned to the stairs. "Crooked."

Dad pressed the button on his torch and shone it at the staircase. It didn't look nearly as crooked as it had felt earlier.

"Let me see," Keisha said, starting up the staircase.

I opened my mouth, planning to tell her to be careful. But Keisha went halfway up, turned and came down again.

"It does feel a little crooked," she said when she got back to where we were standing.

"Does it feel like something's pushing you to the right?" I couldn't help but ask.

Keisha frowned. "Maybe? Let me try again."

She did the stairs once, twice, three times. She was super nice about it, but I could tell she didn't feel anything pushing against her.

Did that mean I had imagined something pushing me?

"Did anything else happen?" Dad asked.

As he turned to face me, it hit me. I'd forgotten something huge.

"I saw the Lady in White too."

As I tapped on the screen to pull up the video I'd taken in the main bedroom, I held my breath. What if the video was like the crooked staircase? What if, when I went to show it to Dad and Keisha, it wasn't there at all?

But luck was on my side. As soon as I started the video, a white, gown-shaped shadow appeared on the screen.

"Yes!"

My voice blared through the little speaker on the bottom of the tablet. I felt heat flood my face as Keisha let out a little laugh next to me. But Dad didn't even crack a smile. He was staring at the screen like it was the best thing he'd ever seen.

"See?" I asked, pointing at the screen. "When I moved, the shadow disappeared, then reappeared again."

"A trick of the lighting?" Dad asked.

"The moon was coming in through the window," I said. "It made a shape on the wall that looked like a gown."

"Let's go and have a look," Dad said.

A couple of minutes later, we were standing in the main bedroom looking out the window.

"What do you see there?" Dad asked.

I stepped to the window. "Trees? Light coming through the trees?"

Dad nodded. "Exactly. The way the light comes through the trees could look like a gown."

My eyes were wide as I looked at him. "That's it!" I exclaimed. "We just solved one of the mysteries. There's no Lady in White after all."

"Unfortunately not," Dad agreed.

I grinned. "Now we just have to work out the phone mystery."

"I think we'll have to postpone that one until tomorrow," Dad said. "It's past our time to wrap up for the night."

I swallowed my groan. I knew I was already lucky to get to stay up late. No way would I complain.

Plus, I couldn't wait to come back tomorrow and see what else I could solve.

Notes

If you've ever heard a noise that you thought was coming from one place when really it was coming from another, you've experienced how sound can travel. But how that happens is kind of complicated.

When a noise is made, it moves from one point to another. It does this through something called sound waves. But what your ears hear is really only the first step. Your brain has to tell you where the sound is coming from.

When sound hits both your ears at the same time, it can be hard for your brain to work out where it's coming from. Big spaces with echoes can make things even more confusing. That's what makes some paranormal investigations so tough. If it's a big, empty castle or an older house without furniture and things in it, the sound has nothing to stop it. It just bounces around and makes things confusing.

CHAPTER 8

The next day, Dad and Keisha set up in the Great Hall bright and early. They had lots and lots of video and audio to go through. I was surprised how much they'd recorded while I'd been upstairs the night before.

Ring-ring-ring.

I was sitting at the table with them when I heard it. But when I turned to look at Dad and Keisha, they both had headphones over their ears and were staring at their screens.

I jumped up and waved, trying to get their attention. Dad seemed startled by my interruption. It was like I'd woken him from a nap. When he was reviewing evidence, the rest of the world didn't exist.

"What's up?" he asked, removing his headphones.

I pointed to the ceiling. "Listen."

Silence.

Dad looked over at Keisha. She removed her headphones too and looked around. "What?"

"Gabby hears something," he said.

"It was a ringing phone," I insisted. This was super frustrating. I'd captured it on my tablet, so I knew I wasn't imagining it.

"Why don't you see if you can find out where it's coming from?" Dad asked.

After last night, I'd assumed Dad would insist I stayed close. But I wasn't about to remind him of that. I grabbed the tablet and darted out of the room.

Ring-ring-ring. Ring-ring-ring.

I'd just entered the study when I heard it
again. This time, it sounded like the ringing
was coming from behind me. But that couldn't
be right. I hadn't heard it at all until I walked
through that door.

Frowning, I turned back towards the door.
The ringing was definitely coming from out
there.

I went back out into the hall, holding the
tablet in front of me to record. The ringing
continued. It sounded like it was coming from
the right, near the bathroom. But when I turned
right, the sound came from behind me. It was
like the sound moved constantly.

What. Was. Happening?

I walked off, making a left turn back towards
the Great Hall. Then the ringing was somehow
to the right of me.

I stopped and took a breath. I was dizzy from

so much turning and walking, turning and walking.

Ring-ring-ring. Ring-ring-ring.

I stopped at the doorway of the Great Hall and looked in at Dad and Keisha. I should ask for help. They could go in one direction, and I could go in another.

"Listen to this!" Keisha called out.

She tapped Dad's arm and pointed at her screen. Dad took off his headphones and listened.

It wasn't the sound on Keisha's screen that had my attention, though. It was the way her voice bounced around when she talked. It sounded almost like . . .

Like it was coming from behind me.

"That's me." Dad laughed. "I sneezed."

Dad's voice carried too. I stepped back and looked around. They'd been working in the study last night, so I hadn't noticed how sound was bouncing around in this big room. That meant the ringing sound I was hearing might bounce around too.

There was a room near by that I hadn't checked yet – the kitchen. It was on the other side of the Great Hall. If the sound was carrying, maybe it was coming from there.

I looked back at Dad and Keisha. *Should I ask them to go with me?*

But Dad still hadn't noticed me standing in the doorway. He'd put his headphones on and turned back to his screen. I didn't want to pull him away right now.

Still recording, I headed for the kitchen. I was halfway there when I heard it again.

Ring-ring-ring.

The sound was faint, and once again sounded like it was coming from behind me, but I made myself keep going forwards. After what I'd realized about the way sound bounced around in here, I didn't want to get confused again.

As I reached the kitchen, the ringing stopped. It was like whoever was making the noise knew I was coming.

The room in front of me looked just like it had on the tour. But I spotted one thing I hadn't noticed before – a long row of small bells hanging way up high near the ceiling. They were attached to the wall with a long, spiral-shaped strip of metal.

Aha! I thought. *Are those bells the ringing I've been hearing?*

Only I didn't see anything attached to ring them. I'd never seen bells mounted to a wall before, though, so I had to check to make sure.

I looked around, my gaze landing on the pair of chairs. Perfect. I grabbed one, dragged it over to the bells, and climbed up. Up close, I could see there were wires that ran from the bells across to the doorway. Could that be how they were ringing?

I reached for the closest bell, stretching my arm as far as it would go. I still couldn't reach. I needed help.

"Dad!" I yelled. "Dad!"

No response. Then I remembered the headphones he'd been wearing. I tapped on the tablet screen and opened the messaging application.

Come to the kitchen, I wrote. *I think I've found something.*

Dad always kept his phone in front of him while he worked. I knew he'd see the screen light up or feel the tablet vibrate.

Sure enough, a few minutes later, I heard footsteps. I put my hand on the wall to balance myself and turned as Dad breezed through the door.

"I'm here," he said. "What's going on?"

I pointed. "Bells. That's what's going on."

Dad's eyes went straight to the bells. "Oh."

"I think that might be the ringing sound I've been hearing," I said, feeling proud of my debunking skills. "But I can't reach them."

Dad reached up and rang each bell, one at a time.

Ring-ring. Ring. Ring-ring.

I listened closely, but the sound wasn't quite right. Not with the first bell or the second or the third. Each sound was different. Some were higher, some were lower, and some were in between.

And none of them sounded like an old phone.

I sighed in frustration. I was so sure I'd found an explanation for the ringing I'd heard.

Dad looked at me. "That's not the same noise," he said.

I shook my head. "Not even close. Maybe

there's something about the way sound carries in the castle? I mean, it is huge."

Dad was still staring up at the bells. "Even if that's the case . . ."

"What's making them ring?" I finished. I had the same question, so it was easy to guess.

Dad nodded. I stepped down from the chair to let him take a closer look at the bells, but I didn't stop investigating. I was busy looking all around the room to see what might've made them ring.

"They're connected!" I said.

At my words, Dad stopped what he was doing and turned to look at me.

"See?" I pointed to the wall, next to the bells. "There are cables and wires."

But when I traced the cable, I found that it was cut. It ended just inches from the bells. There was nothing that would make the bells chime. Nothing but them moving on their own.

Dad pulled his phone out of his pocket and came over to me, typing something as he walked. "They're servant bells," he said, turning the phone so I could see the screen. "A long time ago – probably back when the castle was built – they were used to tell house staff you needed help."

I took Dad's phone. On it was a picture of bells, just like the ones hanging overhead. I read further. According to the website, the cables and pulleys attached to the bells typically ran all through the house.

But the bells in the castle weren't attached to anything. They were just here, with the cables cut. So what was making them ring?

Notes

Servant bells were used in Britain from the late 1700s to the early twentieth century. You'd mostly find them in large houses — homes where you couldn't just shout out when you needed help.

But bells were nothing new. In smaller homes, people used small hand bells. In big houses, the bells were attached to cables, so no matter what room someone was in, a little tug could get the attention of a housekeeper.

You can still see these bells in castles across Europe, as well as in other parts of the world. But many have long been disconnected. Today, you can just pick up your mobile phone and call someone you need, even if that person is in the same house!

CHAPTER 9

I stared at the bells, willing them to ring.
The wind could make things move. Or maybe
it was a change in air pressure. The theories
were at least worth testing. I was determined to
find out why the bells were ringing. If I couldn't
explain it, that might mean it *was* a ghost.

"Nothing?" Keisha asked, sticking her head
in through the doorway. She and Dad were
working their way through the castle, opening
doors and windows to test my theory.

I shook my head. "Nothing."

"I'll keep trying," she said, leaving again.

I stepped back and stared at the bells. They made no noise at all. They just hung there.

I walked over to my backpack and pulled out the tablet. Then I dragged the second chair to the centre of the room. I set up the tablet, pointing it so the camera was on the bells.

There. Now I could do a test.

Next, I walked to the Great Hall and looked around. No windows here. I walked all the way to the door on the other side and peeked out, looking left and right in the corridor. I listened.

No sounds.

I took a right turn towards the study and tried all the windows – none of them opened. I sighed, and looked around the room. There was no exterior door. But there was a front door in the main entrance – of course!

I'd just stepped into the corridor when I heard my name. "Gabby!"

That voice seemed to come from out of nowhere. I stopped and looked around. The bouncing sound was getting annoying.

"Keisha? Is that you?" I called.

Even my voice seemed to come from everywhere. I continued towards the hallway.

"Near the stairs!" Keisha shouted. She was right in front of me, standing between the bottom step and the front door.

I was already walking towards the front door. I had to try this. I pulled the door open and shut it. Then I did it again and again.

Nothing.

I wanted to stamp in frustration. I knew Dad's audience loved it when we couldn't find a reason for something. They tuned in to hear about people experiencing unexplainable things at haunted locations. But the scientist in me loved it when I could prove everything.

I looked at Keisha and shook my head.

"Some things can't be disproved," she reminded me.

"I'm not hearing ringing," Dad said, coming into the hallway.

"I just don't understand what made the bells ring," I said. "There's no logical explanation. And even if there were, that's not the ringing I was hearing."

"It's paranormal," Dad said. "Which just means it can't be explained."

"So Ludwig Castle *is* haunted?" Keisha said.

"I think it's likely," Dad agreed. "But all we can do is tell the audience what we experienced during our investigation – the ringing, the Lady in White, all of it. It's up to listeners to –"

"Decide for themselves," I finished.

"Exactly," Dad said, returning my smile. "Now, let's record the podcast so we can move on to the next location."

Notes

If you're in a spooky place, it might be easy
to imagine a ghost is making something move.
But there are a lot of reasons why objects can
move — and they have nothing to do with ghosts.

Air pressure is an important factor. Just opening
a window or door can change the air pressure in
a house. It can even affect rooms far away on
the other side of the building.

Vibrations can also cause something to move.
It might be someone walking across a room
or it could be a nearby train shaking the ground.
If you're in an area where earthquakes are a
risk, that can shake the ground and make things
shift around a little. Or it could be something you
can't explain. Something paranormal.

CHAPTER 10

I sat at the table in the Great Hall with Dad and Keisha. Today was podcast day. Michelle was at the table with us too. It was time to tell her what we'd found.

"Hi, there," Dad said into the microphone. "I'm Rod, and this is another episode of *Ghost Search*. Joining us tonight is Michelle Wagner, the owner of Ludwig Castle, and our host on this investigation."

"Hello," Michelle said. "I hear you caught some interesting stuff."

"Oh, yes." Dad smiled at me, then shifted back to the microphone. "The biggest mystery we solved was the Lady in White. My daughter, Gabby, was the one who uncovered the truth." He turned to me. "Gabby, tell us what you saw."

"I was in the main bedroom when I saw the shape of a woman on the wall," I told Michelle. "It looked like the skirt of a gown that went way out. At the top was a shape that looked like a head. But then . . ."

I moved over so Michelle could see the tablet screen too. Then I tapped play to start the video.

"Is this what you've seen?" I asked.

"That's her!" Michelle exclaimed. "The Lady in White! That's exactly what I've seen. You got her on video."

Dad leaned into his microphone. "For listeners, the video we're looking at shows a clear outline of a woman on the wall," he explained. "It glows, like from a light. We'll post the video on our site so you can examine it for yourselves."

I looked back at Michelle. Her eyes were wide, and she had a huge smile on her face. I almost hated to let her down. But I had to tell her what I'd found.

"I thought it was Grace too," I admitted. "At first." I pointed to the screen. "But see how the shape changes as I move round the room? It's the light coming through the window."

"We got a photo of it too." Dad turned his screen around. On it was the image we'd taken showing the way the outline of the trees looked like the shape of a dress. "The dress people see is the result of the way the light comes through the trees."

"We'll put all these pictures on the website," I said. That's what we did with the evidence we collected, especially visual evidence, so listeners could see for themselves.

"But –" Michelle opened her mouth and closed it again. "As I said on the tour, my employees have seen and heard things throughout the house."

Dad spoke then. "As our listeners know, just because we didn't see or hear anything doesn't mean nothing's here. It just means we didn't experience it in the course of our investigation."

"There's more," I added.

Dad nodded. "The ringing telephone."

"Did you hear it?" Michelle looked from me to Dad, her eyes wide with excitement.

"We did," I said. "I actually managed to get it on audio."

From the other side of the table, Keisha pressed play on the audio recording I'd captured on the tablet.

Ring-ring-ring. The sound played clearly through the speakers.

"That's it!" Michelle said. She clapped her hands a little, practically bouncing in her chair with excitement. "That's what I hear all the time too."

I nodded. "For a while, I was convinced the bells in your kitchen were responsible for the sound," I said. "Did you know they were there?"

Michelle nodded. "The servant bells. Yes, they were there when I bought the property, but the wires were already disconnected," she said. "I presumed they couldn't be making the noise."

"You were right," I admitted. "We tested the bells ourselves, and the sound isn't the same. We couldn't find any reason to explain the sound I heard. The sound we *all* heard on the video."

"We also couldn't find any reason the bells would be ringing at all," Dad said. "The wires are disconnected, as you said."

That brought a big smile to Michelle's face. "That's good news. Is that all?"

I looked at Dad. He nodded. This was my story to tell.

"Something weird happened to me on the stairs," I said. "I wanted to see if it has ever happened to anyone else."

"You felt like you were being pushed," Michelle said.

I don't know how long I stared at her, my mouth open. "How did you know that?" I asked.

"It's happened before," she replied.

"Why didn't you tell us that?" I asked.

Michelle shrugged. "It's only happened a couple of times, and never to me. I just assumed it was because the stairs aren't level.

I know we should do something about them, but I don't want to take away from the castle's spooky feeling."

I smiled a little. "It is spooky." After my experiences, even I had to admit that. "But it can still be that way without trying so hard to make things scary for guests."

Michelle nodded. "You're right," she said. "I should let the castle speak for itself." She looked at Dad and Keisha. "This is one clever debunker you have here."

"Yes, she is," Dad said, smiling at me. "Gabby is the best team member I could ask for, in fact. She not only researches the hauntings, but she does it without judgement. She knows, like we do, that listeners have to decide for themselves. But the truth is more important than stories."

Dad said all that, but it wasn't his words that made me smile. It was the pride in his eyes. And that meant more to me than anything I could imagine.

He finished off the podcast, but I barely heard it. All I could think about was how far I'd come this summer. And we had plenty more adventures to come.

Notes

Ghost sightings – along with UFOs and monsters in the woods – are sometimes called "paranormal activity". Paranormal simply means "beyond normal". If something is paranormal, it can't be explained by science.

Often, paranormal investigators go into a place wanting to get to the truth of a haunting. If strange things – smells, sounds and sights – can be explained, then a place isn't haunted. If they can't be explained, it's paranormal. Or maybe it's just that someone like me hasn't come along and found the real truth – yet!

CASE RECAP:

LOCATION: Ludwig Castle

HAUNTING: Lady in White; mysterious ringing phone

CONCLUSION: Some things can't be explained. My spotting of a Lady in White upstairs was a trick of the lighting. We couldn't find that same trick of lighting anywhere else in the castle, so I'm doubtful that there's a real Lady in White being seen there.

Then there was the push on the stairs. Slanted or not, I know I felt like I was being pushed. It would help if the owner straightened the stairs. At least then, people would know that what they're feeling has nothing to do with the steps being crooked.

I still can't work out the ringing. If I hadn't heard it with my own ears, I'd say people were imagining it. But I also have it on recording – and it's not the servant bells. Is it Grace calling her husband? I can't say. As I said, there are some mysteries that can't be solved. And I have to be okay with that.

Discussion questions

1. Gabby and her dad spend the night investigating a supposedly haunted castle. Would you want to spend a night doing the same? Why or why not?

2. The stairs in the castle were crooked, but at the same time, Gabby felt like she was being pushed. Do you think she imagined being pushed? Or was something really pushing her?

3. The servant bells were used to get the attention of people on the other side of the house. How do you get the attention of your family when you're in the house together?

Writing prompts

1. Write about what you think it would be like to live in a castle in the 1800s. How do you think life was different back then? Are there any ways it might be similar to life today?

2. The painting of Grace makes Gabby wonder about the woman's story. Look at an old painting and write a story to go with it. What was the person thinking when the portrait was painted? What was happening in the scene?

3. Gabby learns that there are some things she can't explain. Have you ever experienced something you couldn't explain? How did it make you feel?

Glossary

authentic when a person, object or emotion is genuinely what it seems to be

debunk expose the falseness of something

evidence information, items and facts that help prove something is true or false

experience either seeing or participating in something

investigate gather facts in order to discover as much as possible about an event or a person

lantern light or candle with a case or a frame to protect it

legend story passed down through the years that may not be completely true

paranormal having to do with an unexplained event that has no scientific explanation

patent official document that gives an inventor the sole right to make, use or sell their invention for a certain number of years

phenomenon something very unusual or remarkable

podcast online audio show available for download to a computer or other device

producer someone who prepares a public presentation such as a film, TV show or podcast

researcher someone who studies a subject to discover new information

telegraph machine that uses electronic signals to send messages over long distances

ABOUT THE AUTHOR

photo credit: Taylor Alexander Photography

Stephanie Faris is the author of the Piper Morgan chapter book series, as well as the novels *30 Days of No Gossip*, *25 Roses* and *The Popularity Code*. She loves to travel and always takes a ghost tour when she's in a new town!

ABOUT THE COVER ARTIST

Chloe Friedlein is an illustrator and visual development artist. She received her Bachelor of Fine Arts and now works as a freelance illustrator. At weekends, she enjoys playing softball with her husband, Joshua, and catering to the every need of her art assistant – also known as her cat, Furguson.